i

c

o

p

e

M

DISCARDED

*for John A. Jackson*

# BLACK CLOUD

JULIET ESCORIA

To view the video component for each story,
please go to the *Black Cloud* Vimeo channel:

**https://vimeo.com/channels/blackcloud**

# RESENTMENT

# FUCK CALIFORNIA

That was the summer the waters in the lagoon swelled, and the gnats and mosquitoes swarmed in black clouds. We would sit on the beach in his rusty lawn chairs, the nylon threads turning white before snapping. We drank cases of beer, first cold and then no longer cold and then warm, out of cans hidden in paper bags, and the bug bites popped red on our heels. The day turned into night, and we rolled from the chairs onto the sand, not really minding the bugs, and I whispered to him, "I love you," for the very first time, and I meant it.

I thought I meant it.

The days grew shorter and the mosquito bites

healed. That was the winter the kelp uprooted itself, splaying on the sand in rusty, rotting piles, making the beach stink of death. We went down there one night, hopeful, but I could only stand it for ten minutes. Right before we left—he didn't want us to go—I said to him, "It just seems like the ocean is trying to get at us," and he smiled at me like I was a morbid and silly child. He was one of those that came here from somewhere else, and saw everything as great, waking just about every day to declare it a beautiful morning. Fuck California, I said under my breath. And also: fuck you.

We took his lawn chairs back where they came from, to the deck at his house, where we could see a little of downtown and the bay, which was polluted, but mostly we were looking at the airport.

This was also the winter I couldn't get warm. The sea air dug into my bones, it seemed, and wouldn't get out. There really was no other explanation. My skin was thinner, more transparent, than before, and my veins seemed much more blue. My arms and chest looked like maps, maps with a whole lot of rivers. I drank to melt away the chill. I couldn't tell you why he drank, all I know was he did it too.

In the kitchen before dinner one night, it turned out I'd had too much and I fainted. One moment I had my elbows on the counter and the next I was a sloppy puddle on the floor. I'd hit the tile smack on my cheekbone. In the morning I had a black eye. "Looks like you talked back," he joked. I pretended to laugh, but really I was thinking about how his dumb jokes made me sick.

Our last night together, and we went to the sex shop to buy whippets. I hadn't done those things since I was fifteen. We went out on the patio and sat in the chairs, our big pint glasses forming rings on the old wooden planks of the deck. The empty cartridges made a pile at our feet, silver and glinting spent bombs. The iciness of the gas brought blisters to our fingers. And our thoughts—they stilled before they burst, and then we laughed, and then we laughed.

It smelled like gasoline because of the airport, and looked nothing at all like the beach. But if I sucked enough nitrous and shook my head the right way, I could trick myself into thinking the roar of the jets was that of the waves, and the lights on the landing strip were, in fact, stars.

# CONFUSION

# THE OTHER KIND OF MAGIC

## I.

You work in a nightclub, in coat check. The club is three stories, and well drinks are twelve dollars. This is in Manhattan, right near the Williamsburg Bridge. The coat check is on the top floor, which is closed in by a glass ceiling. The lights on the bridge look like they are there specifically to impress all the girls in their tight neon dresses and all the boys in their polo shirts, as they get fucked up on bottle service and molly and sing along to that Jay-Z song.

The coat check job is three nights a week, Thursday through Saturday. You make more in a night at this job than you do in two weeks at your "real" job, which is adjuncting English. To do *that* job, you need an advanced degree. To do *this* job, you need to put on a lot of make-up, a slutty outfit, and look younger than your twenty-nine years. Nothing adds up in New York, and you like that.

One of the owners has a thing for you. He stands there and stares at you from the end of the hallway, wearing his dark velvet suits. He's mean to everyone, swearing and brooding, but for you he brings cupcakes from the kitchen. You smoke together on the deck when it's slow. He tells you about his girlfriend, who is seven years younger than you and covered in tattoos. They fight a lot. You ask him if they tell each other 'I love you' and he says yes, but it's just something he says. He asks you if you do the same with your boyfriend, and you say yes, but you actually mean it. You tell him how nice your boyfriend is, how smart and funny and talented.

You tell him how happy you are together and how it's assumed you'll marry, but even you hear the catch in your voice. It starts to rain, and the cabs drive by in whispers.

## II.

The tattooed girl and the owner break up. You and your boyfriend stay together.

## III.

Christmas happens. You go to your boyfriend's home for the second year in a row and his parents have a fire lit and it is snowing and they are happy to see you. The two of you sleep in his childhood bed and you feel so safe in his arms and they are around you like a blanket but all you want to do is go outside so you can shiver. There is something deeply wrong at your core and you know it and have always known it but he doesn't see it yet.

## IV.

In the new year, you wait in the basement, which is dark and smelly because this is the floor where the clientele get the freakiest. Apparently it is not unusual to watch some girl get fingerbanged on the dance floor. At least that's what the bartenders say.

It is five AM. You have four hundred dollars rolled up, in the zippered part of your pocketbook. You sip a whiskey and ginger and watch yourself in the mirror behind the bar. Your make-up and hair are still perfect, and you look slinky and you could totally pass for twenty-two.

The idea is you are waiting to take a car back to Brooklyn with your friend, a bartender who's still busy cashing out. The truth is you are waiting for the right time to slip away with the owner. His name is Jim.

"How much longer?" you say to your friend as she counts the bills under her breath. "I'm getting really tired."

"I haven't added the tips yet." This means she won't be ready for another thirty minutes, at least, which is perfect. She starts back at one, because you made her lose count. You finish your drink and tell her you'll just go home alone.

Around the corner on Delancey, and he is waiting for you in the back of a black car. You get in. He takes you to breakfast. You order waffles, with whipped cream and strawberries, but are too nervous to eat much. He looks old in the diner light, which brings out the bags under his eyes. But the irises are very blue, and his lips look soft.

He kisses you for the first time in front of that diner. It is cold, and you forgot your gloves, and the puffs of both your breaths intermingle in clouds. He gives you a twenty to take a cab home.

Your boyfriend stirs in his sleep as you enter the bedroom. He is shirtless and illuminated by the hall light. "I tried to stay up for you," he says, his voice thick with sleep. "What time is it?"

"Six," you say, although it's seven, and the lie worms in your gut. "Some of us got breakfast."

After you take off your make-up and clothes, you get in bed next to him. His heart beats steady and strong. You wrap your arms around him and whisper *I love you* into his ear, and you mean it so much you start to cry.

# V.

Your boyfriend takes a long weekend upstate, with
his friend who has a recording studio in the shed.
You can't go because you have work.

# VI.

On Saturday, you stand in the basement again, waiting for your friend. Jim is next to you, talking about
nothing in a low voice. He stands too close. You're
worried someone will see so you pull away, but he
moves in again and cups your ass in his hands. You
swear at him, but you aren't actually angry.

In the cab home, your friend asks, "What's going
on with you and Jim?"

"Nothing," you say, and because you're bad at lying you stare out the window.

## VII.

On Sunday night, you pack a bag and ride to Port Authority. You're wearing a black dress and high boots with fishnets because that's what he told you to wear, and you are wicked. He's waiting for you outside like he said he'd be, smoking his Marlboro Reds. He smiles when he sees you. He never smiles. It is weird to see him happy.

## VIII.

You sit in the back of the bus. The floor lights are purple, and people are already slumped and sleeping against the windows. The lights of Lincoln

Tunnel go by so fast that it feels like a zoetrope. You go underground as yourself, and as the lights flick by you spin into a cheater.

It is late and the world is quiet and New Jersey looks pretty in the dark. You ask Jim to tell you about being a teenager in New York in the eighties. He tells you it was a different city, with all that crime. He tells you about sitting in the back of CBGBs. He tells you the kids at the clubs would wear lace and eyeliner and dance to Siouxsie Sioux, and everyone was brilliant and fabulous, and there was no bottle service or fake lines out front. His voice is soft and it feels like he is speaking fairy tales. You look out the window into the darkness, and your secret is inside you and you feel sordid but also happy and you think to yourself, this is my life.

# IX.

In Atlantic City, he wants to play poker and have you sit by his side. You think about all the girls that came before you, five and ten years under your age, and how they all probably said yes, but watching men fling around money sounds boring so you refuse. You've never been interested in acting like anyone's trophy—which is one reason why he likes you. You're older so you do what you want.

Instead, you go straight to the room. It is nothing fancy, and for a moment you are disappointed. But then he kisses you hard, and lowers you onto the bed, and reaches up your skirt and pulls down your thong without pause and without asking. For the second time that night he smiles, and then he enters you.

## X.

Afterwards, you stare up at the ceiling, naked, no covers over your body. He pulls you into his chest, and he smells entirely unfamiliar.

You ask Jim to tell you a story, a request you used to ask your boyfriend when it was late but you still couldn't sleep. Your boyfriend always said no, his excuse being he has no way with words, so you stopped asking.

Jim is a different man. He strokes your hair, and tells you about the homeless people on the streets of Miami Beach, and how he paid them in malt liquor to do security at his club. You close your eyes, and you smile, and soon you are asleep. When you wake, Jim is gone, busy losing his money at the casinos. He comes back in a very bad mood. The afternoon bus ride home is quiet and sullen, too bright, and there are no city fairy tales on the way.

## XI.

There are two more bus trips and hotel rooms. Each trip goes pretty much the same. Each morning you wake up alone and he's at the casinos, and he never picks up his cell phone and it all makes you feel so helpless and pale and when you ride back to the city there's never anything to say. Spring is coming, and coat check season will be over soon.

## XII.

You leave your laptop open on the couch and go get a haircut. While you're gone, your boyfriend reads your messages. The worst one is the most recent.

*i love my boyfriend but i think i might be starting to love you too*

You have no idea why you even typed that.

There is a fight. In it, you become single and homeless. In the morning, you call Jim and you are crying and you tell him the truth, which is that your heart is destroyed. You want to tell him it's his fault, but it isn't—this was all broken by you.

He tells you to pack your things and take the train up to 59th and Lexington. You can live with him. You won't even have to work. Something in the way he's phrasing things tells you this is exactly what he wanted all along.

You think about it, what it would be like to live in Manhattan, how there would be dinners out and manicures, jewelry, and fancy shoes. You'd sleep til noon, every day. You'd sit at the window, and stare down at lights that looked like Oz, and you'd be there, trapped and pretty, a golden life charmed, but one not meant for a girl like you.

# APATHY

# REDUCTION

This was the old days, back when you could go down to Tijuana without a passport. It started with us lying on my bed and snorting ketamine. He had a co-worker with a sick grandmother who lived down there; the co-worker would visit and come back with a few vials of the stuff. My not-yet-boyfriend and I cooked one down in the kitchen of my shitty little studio, pouring it into the previously unused glass casserole dish my mom had given me to make lasagna. "Lasagnas are nutritious," she had said, "and they freeze well." We added a dash of vanilla and cooked it for twenty minutes on low, like baking cookies. The crystals formed pale yellow, and once we had them chopped up and snorted, the drip tasted like chemicals and candy.

My guy wasn't much besides his job—he was a programmer, Linux—but I didn't know that yet. Hard to have foresight when you're spending nights on your back with the room throbbing inside your ears, when your version of an activity is clumsy fucking. It all sounds so stupid and misguided, one giant act of folly, us beginning our relationship like that.

But we'd lay on my sheets sweating, not moving, and I'd look at him. I'd look right into him, and I knew we were cut from the same sheer cloth. Apart, on our own, we were pale and flimsy, but on top of each other we gained shape, could almost stand straight up. It made sense, and it wasn't just the drugs.

Three weeks in, and he brought over his laptop

and clothes. He had lived with his boss, who was a Christian, and spending nights alone made him feel suicidal. We could never sleep, and the early mornings were spent staring at our computer screens like they were mirrors, like if we looked hard enough we could find the outline of ourselves.

The grandmother in Tijuana died, so we stopped baking and did coke instead. Sometimes we argued, but our words were always half-hearted and blanched. He went to work and constructed code. I waited tables and collected tips. Sometimes I'd wake up at dawn and find myself tangled in his arms, one of my yellow hairs stuck to his eyebrow. We got nosebleeds. We made lasagna. I got pregnant.

He had told me he was sterile, that his stepfather had thrown a can of beans at his nuts when he was nine. I asked what kind and he said, "Refried," so we did it without a condom and had been doing so ever since. He was good enough to not ask if it was really his. I was dumb enough to not wonder if he'd been lying all along.

I was taking a night class, English, at the J.C. Sometimes I'd get all the way to campus only to keep on driving, ditching class to eat Taco Bell. On the occasions I did make it into the classroom, I usually fell asleep on my desk, the teacher's voice a bland lullaby. Pregnancy turned me into a baby myself—all I wanted was to eat and sleep. I'd come home from class and collapse on the bed. Sometimes my boyfriend would hold me. "My babies," he'd say, stroking my hair.

We saved up the money for the abortion by the second month. I hadn't wanted one, because I liked feeling it grow, but he convinced me that this was unwise. Only when we got to Planned Parenthood, the doctor said there was no heartbeat. She examined me and, with her gloved, lubricated fingers still inside, said I must have expelled it on my own. The word "expelled" made me feel like a snake, like something that had slipped out of its own skin.

He, strangely enough, was mad at me. "How could you not notice something like that falling out?" Like he thought there'd be a bloody baby squirming in the toilet, and I was too stupid to pluck it from the water.

We fell into a state of nothingness after that. I spent the days after the appointment staring through the bedroom window, out at our view of the alley. Sometimes the haze would turn the sky scarlet at sunset and the birds would perch on the power lines in blackened silhouettes, but usually I must admit that I was staring at nothing at all. He would come home from work and find me there, silent and smelling of blood. He tried to kiss me, on my cheek, on my forehead, turning my face toward his and placing his mouth over mine, silently demanding I kiss back, but it was always him kissing me, and me just being there.

# GUILT

# HEROIN STORY

The heroin story I know best is about a couple. I met the boy a long time ago. He told me he was single but that was a lie. We slept together for a while, off and on, despite him not being single. We fought a lot and hated each other sometimes, until one day I looked at him and realized he had become my very close friend. Once I smoked some DMT because someone gave it to me, and it made me giggle and I couldn't stand up from the bed I was sitting on. I had a dream, and in the dream I was a lot older. I knew I had aged because my skin felt light like paper but the inside of me was solid and dark. The sun was low in the sky and thick yellow like tree sap, that gorgeous time of day right before the sun begins to set. I was with the boy and he was older too—a man now—and we were married; there were vines growing up the fence and the leaves were buzzing with new growth and his skin was warm under my fingers as I kissed him. I looked in his eyes, the man in the dream, and couldn't believe that I had known, and hated, and loved this person for so long. In him I could see who I was, who I had been.

But the problem with DMT is it makes you dream and the dream seems so real, but it lasts so short and goes away so fast. I was back in the bedroom and the light dragged trails.

I hadn't known the girl as long. The boy had to wait for us to be just friends before he could introduce me to her, because he'd been the girl's the entire time we were sleeping together, plus a year or two before that. It turned out that when I'd met him she'd recently smashed out his car windows with her bare fists, and also given him genital warts. She told me later, much later when we too were friends, that she'd known she had warts but she wanted to keep it a secret from him, just to have one, something that was not his but would be soon, like a baby. She cut them off (there were three, triplets) with a pair of manicure scissors and taped them in her journal like they were old scabs. When he asked her what the cuts were from she said she was fucked up and shaving. She said it was a hard spot to shave. He didn't pass the genital warts on to me, but still, it was a pretty shitty thing for her to do.

Oh, but I didn't mean for it to go like this. This story was supposed to be them: the couple, two people, symmetrical, no piece of me. But with every breath and every step, I find myself more entwined with them. We are braided around each other like snakes.

Some days I don't wake up till the sun's going down and my role in things weighs down so darkly it near chokes me.

Anyway. Here is the story of the two of them, the short version. He started heroin and then quit. They got together. They fought a lot. They broke up. She started shooting. They got back together. He started shooting again. They both quit. They broke up. They started and stopped many more times, both with the drugs and each other. Eventually they realized that no matter what they would still be unhappy, and this made them perfect for each other. They were soulmates now. They quit doing drugs for a long time, and stayed unhappy and in love. They lived, and when they were very old they started shooting again, for no reason at all. And then they died.

# DISGUST

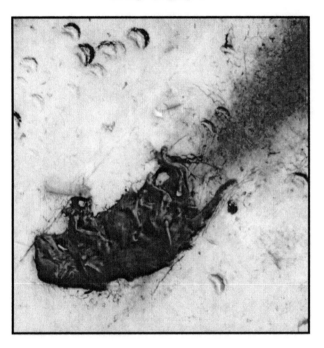

# THE SHARPEST PART OF HER

My mother had been clean for most of her pregnancy so no one suspected what was to come. True, no family had come while she was in labor, or even after I was born. No father, either. But it was New York, it was 1982, and this was common enough.

It took three days, she told me. Three days of listening to me scream. I didn't shut up, except to sleep, and those intervals were not enough for her. She held me, she fed me, she rocked me, she sang—she did everything she was supposed to—yet all I did was scream.

I suppose that's why there should be two parents, she said, one to relieve the other to save them both from going nuts.

But there weren't two parents; there was only her. My father may have been a photographer, a club promoter, or another model, and it didn't matter which, because each of the potential liaisons-turned-sperm donors were 'scumbags' and 'idiots.'

Not my mother, of course. My mother, the blond beauty, was now a young single mother, and she couldn't handle the pressure. Less than seventy-two hours after she left the hospital, her old coke dealer was on the phone. I needed to get my figure back, she told me, I needed to find some joy.

Finding joy in a straw, it's always stunned me how little her justifications made sense. But I guess the strangest part of the whole situation was that she told me at all.

Therapists have looked at me, their eyes pleadingly wet and round, and said that growing up in a household like mine must have not felt that strange because it was all I knew. I can't say this was true for me, not quite, because I do remember the pliancy of things, how nothing ever felt like it was happening at the right time or would stay standing up. My mother would not sleep; she would bake for me, cookies and pies, she would sew up the holes in my clothes, make me stuffed teddy bears, bring home sparkly things from photo shoots for me to play with. Always laughing and singing through her shiny white teeth. We went to the parks at dawn and had picnics, jelly sandwiches with the crusts cut off. The leaves on the trees were new and green and so impossibly small like the toys of dolls; the pink lemonade in my wax cup was the same color as the edges of brightening sky. "Pinkies up!" my mother said, sticking her finger and elbow up and out. I tried to imitate her and failed—holding the cup was pretty much the pinnacle of my motor skills—and she laughed and tickled my stomach, spilling lemonade on my dress, but my dress was pink too and my mother was happy so a little bit of juice didn't matter.

And then she slept, she cried, her mouth was a slit, I was hungry and so I poured myself cereal but I spilled the milk and then ran into the street for fear my mother would hit me. She would hit me. Three hours later, my mother retrieved me, her face puffy and tear-stained but smiling, from Mrs. Jenkins's down the hall. She took me by the hand, told me how worried she was. Mrs. Jenkins clucked her tongue, said how silly children were, gave a sympathetic look to my mother. Then my mother took me across the hall, closed the door, turned on the record player, Jane's Addiction (I still hate that band), and then she hit me. First she was just thwacking me on my thighs and butt, this was spanking and she said it was okay, Perry Farrell was whining about summertime, but I started to cry, she turned up the music and then she hit me across the mouth. *Shut up*, she said to me, *Shut up, you ugly little brat.* My lip began to bleed and then swell. I wasn't allowed to go to school for a week, even though my mother was still getting gigs then and gone most days. All week, the TV was my babysitter.

She would take me to the magazine stands whenever a photo she had been in was published. Sometimes she'd be out all night, and come in with a slam of the door, and then she'd wake me up and make me put on my sneakers. I could feel her excitement as she took my hand and pulled me into the street. It's so bright! she shrilled in my ear, once we were on the sidewalk. We went down the street, down the blocks where the concrete sparkled like fairies. I looked up at my mother, her straightened, highlighted hair, its ends in tangles, her eyes sooty with eyeliner, the faint lines settling in like dust around her mouth.

At the newsstand, my mother bought me candy. She slit open the package and poured some into my hand. I ate them as she tore through the pages of the magazine. The bright colors of the candy in my hand, and then in my mouth, were too vivid to belong there, but my mother had given them to me so I ate them anyway. They were chewy and stuck to my teeth.

Here it is, she said, and then handed me the magazine. A close-up of her face. It looked like my mother but it didn't. She was wearing all black; her hair hung down around her, smooth, golden, and liquid. Her mouth was open, and her teeth, underneath her parted pink lips, looked sharp and scary. Feline.

"Is that you?" I said, and pointed to the lady in the magazine. I looked up at my mother, dirty and buzzing in the bright morning light. Two images, the same but different, like looking into a smear-stained mirror.

"Yes, of course it's me," she said, "give me that." She ripped the magazine from my hands, closed it shut so fast it made a slapping sound, and slid it into her purse.

Things really began to slip once her teeth started getting fucked up. The phone in the kitchen rang less. My mother was home more. Her front two teeth were grey, hiding in shadows. The dates, the calls, the jobs, the absences: the duration between them all grew wider. The front teeth's vigor returned; they glowed yellow like streetlamps, but it was a tricky surge and didn't last long. Soon they shrank, grew dark and withered.

You might think that because my mother was home more, because she had more time for me, the love she shared with me would grow. But it was like her teeth. What was once only faintly flawed became something dark and rotting. I missed school a lot then. What made it worse was I was rarely allowed to go into the kitchen, where she was. Where she sat with her cigarettes, glass and paper, always something being drawn to her mouth that wasn't me.

The phone began ringing again. I thought this was good, except she kept hanging up without speaking. Ring-bang, ring-bang. I counted them while I watched the TV. Thirty-six. Thirty-six rings til she picked up the phone. Jesus fucking Christ, what is it, she yelled. My kid is trying to sleep.

The digital clock read 6:23. It was light out.

I crept into the doorway of the kitchen, low so she wouldn't see. She cradled the phone on her neck, lit one of her long white cigarettes. She exhaled through the black gap of her mouth. That could work, she said to the phone.

Chuck was over a lot now. That's what he told me to call him. He slept in my mother's bed sometimes, snoring real low and rumbly, but that, of course, wasn't as bad as the other noises that slid under the door. Chuck's muscles bulged in odd places and his arms and chest seemed thin-skinned like chicken meat, one bicep adorned with a tattooed rose. His teeth were dark and small like my mother's.

It was Chuck who got me out of there. Right when my mother's looks really started to spiral, right when her cheeks began to sink into her face. He was sleeping there too often, and where he slept, his clients followed. Can't raise a little girl in a crack house. I wasn't even sad when I left because they let me bring my stuffed cat and Ninja Turtle toothbrush.

I was twenty-three when my mother cleaned up. The social workers and therapists, they all told me I should talk to her. Forgiveness leads to healing, they said, and I agreed.

Like them, I wanted to see things between us sewn up. I was mature enough to know that the first phone call might be filtered through awkward pauses, and it was. I went to the resulting lunch date—at a diner, Formica tables and big dirty windows—fully prepared that some residual anger might sneak up in my chest, and it did. A fist rising up like indigestion from the moment I saw her from across the restaurant, looking sad-eyed into a cup of coffee at a corner booth. She was no longer beautiful. I saw that, and I will admit this is when the fist receded. Now she actually looked like she could be somebody's mother. She was mine.

I thought she wouldn't recognize me. It had been so long. I had it all rehearsed in my head, how I would stand over her and say, *It's me, Mom. It's your daughter*, and she would look confused and surprised. But she saw me and stood up. There were tears in her eyes, and she hugged me tight, and it all felt so Hallmark melodrama it made me squeamish. I tried to not shut down, to not shut her out, to not get cold and steely on the inside; I really wanted to give it all a fair chance. But it's hard when your mother is still wearing the same perfume, the same one that, when you smell it on strange women in the subway, still makes you think of coming home from school to the lights off and the blinds drawn and that weird burnt chemical smell heavy in the air.

She called me today. It's been six years since we first "reunited," and I have to give it to her—she tries. Sometimes I can hear the questions in between her silences on the phone: *Why won't you forgive me?* But I don't have to worry. I know she's too afraid to ask.

# *SPITE*

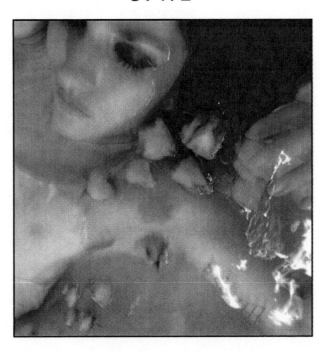

# GLASS, DISTILLED

I started using meth the way most people do: one day our dealer was out of everything else. Things were different after that. We only ever did meth anymore. Adam was in charge of how and when we got high. Not having my own drugs bothered me sometimes, but not enough to figure out how to make the money to get my own. Most days, seemed good enough to have someone so obsessed with me that he'd pay for this life. He must have thought if he kept me high, I might love him in return. But things had changed, and I wasn't sure he meant much to me anymore.

Our drug dealer Mike was past the acceptable age of someone in his line of work. He lived in a pay-by-the-month motel down the street. Bald, over-weight, and a diabetic amputee. To get the drugs, we had to sit in his room and listen to stories about his pathetic life. He enlisted in the navy at the age of seventeen, got kicked out thirteen years later for the habit he'd picked up. It was unclear whether it was the diabetes, the drugs, or the war that caused the loss of his arm. He waved the stump, like it still ended in a hand, as he told us how he got married to a Taiwanese chick overseas. How in quick succession she gave birth to two sons, then asked for divorce the same month she got naturalized. He hadn't seen his sons in six years now. Mike always talked about how he was getting his kids back soon, but of course soon never came because soon never does. As he said this, his face went blank and he covered his stump with his one good hand, in a way that almost eclipsed the deformity.

Mike and Adam always talked about fish. Mike liked both snorkeling and fishing, back when his body was whole and the sadness hadn't yet crept in, back when he was still a young man and in the navy. Adam had a huge tank of fresh waters—cichlids, three puffers, and an eel. He'd picked up the hobby around the same time my emotions slipped away. Both little things that needed to be fed.

The hallways and rooms in the motel were heavy with the ghosts of its tenants. Mike's room held a twin bed, a mini-fridge, and all of his shitty clothes. There was no kitchen, no bathroom—Mike had to share a single toilet and shower stall with the rest of the derelicts in the motel. There was a nightstand, all flimsy plastic wood and carved-in graffiti, and on it rested three photos: the two sons, a bleeding Jesus, and a young Mike, still with all four limbs, holding up a marlin, his face aglow from holding that big life on a string.

After we met with Mike, we'd go home and smoke the stuff and then usually we'd have sex. Adam liked to tie me up and hit me with his hands, sometimes a belt, sometimes a crop we'd bought at the pet supply store—because crops meant for horses were cheaper than those meant for people—before fucking me. This was the only kind of sex I could manage anymore; the old soft kind left me feeling both bored and alone. When we tried to fuck normal, always on Adam's volition, I'd lay silent, flat on my back, Adam's chest heaving over me, as he looked at my face while I stared at the fish in the tank that illuminated the room from the foot of our bed. The fish's eyes were blank and their mouths opened and closed with nothing coming out. When I looked at them, it seemed like we were the exact same kind of being.

At first it was enough to have my ass turn red, but

soon the effectiveness faded and I needed him to bruise me in order to feel any sort of thing at all. One time he slapped me so hard I got a black eye, and the pleasure surged from the weight of his hand. Even looking in the mirror later, watching the bruise that cupped my eye as it waned from blue to yellow in the passing days, made me feel almost like I loved him again, almost like his name was still carved inside my heart. But the black eye scared Adam off. Said he was a nice Catholic boy; nice Catholic boys don't beat their women like that, even if and when they ask for it. I'd wanted to point out the incongruity, that nice Catholic boys don't smoke drugs like these either but sometimes, when you're high, making words proves more of an effort than it's worth.

One day we decided to do an experiment. I was at school, and, like usual, Adam went to Mike's after he got off work. I was tired when I got home but felt better when I saw the little baggies sitting there on our coffee table, the tiny crystals just gleaming and waiting. Except there was another bag too, this one pinkie mice, their flesh wrinkled and naked, tiny eyes still shut into slits. Adam said he wanted to try feeding them to the fish. Said he'd read on the internet that sometimes puffers were into that kind of thing, that this type of fish had teeth.

We smoked the stuff, and I settled back into my bones again. Adam let me dangle the first mouse above the water. He sat next to me, his knee pressing into my thigh.

The fish swam up. The cichlids were first, and they sniffed but then quickly darted away, bored. The puffers, though—they knew what was going on. One nibbled delicately, first at the tail and then at the arm. The mouse hung there, suspended in my fingers, pale trails of blood trickling into the water from where the limbs used to be. The baldness, the incompleteness, reminded me of Mike. Suddenly I almost wished he was here, telling us sad stories and cupping his incomplete wrist.

Soon the other fish smelled the blood and the three of them ate that baby mouse in no time at all. They bit off the head, then gnawed into the stomach. The guts looked like porcelain miniatures, but the fish ate them before they separated completely so I never got to see them sink into the water. As I fed them the second mouse, the fish almost jumped out the tank. By then I could see the change in their eyes: no longer flat and empty, now charged with the thick beat of a new electricity. They'd consumed something living, and suddenly their tiny world was no longer closed in by glass walls.

# REVENGE

# HURRICANE SEASON

Itchy in November, right before Thanksgiving. It was my first winter sober, when you were living on the top floor of that six-story apartment building overlooking the river, back before the neighborhood was converted into condos.

"Hurricane season," you said when you saw me looking out your window in that blank way. "When the temperatures drop, us drunks get restless."

Your hands got busy stacking up wood in the fireplace. I'd seen people who had come into the same meetings every week suddenly stop showing up, seen the way that the ones who did come back would raise their hands, announcing their day

counts, differently this time. "I've got five days."
"Nineteen days." "I've got forty-one days back,"
they'd say, the "back" added to show that this
wasn't their first time at the rodeo. It didn't look
like it was any easier, though: their hands shook
like any newcomer's, their eyes wandered the
rooms the same way, rabid.

I still didn't know anyone in those days, so I
couldn't ask them why they left, or how it felt to
come back. I wouldn't have known about what was
going on at all if you hadn't explained it to me. You
said that no one talked to me because they were
jealous that I was pretty, but that didn't make sense
to me, not even then. There were other pretty girls
in the program, and they had friends. I thought the
difference between me and them must have been
you. Well, at least, that you didn't help. But it must
have looked worse from your corner: you were

twice my age, with fifteen years of sobriety, yet you were there dating me, the fragile newcomer. You always swore up and down that this was the first time you'd done such a thing, but I doubted you. Doubted that this was your first time with the so-called thirteenth step—the one where you initiate a newcomer by fucking them.

I pressed my fingers against the glass. Your window was double-paned, but it still felt bone-cold. You struck a match, held it up to crumpled newspaper.

"So what do I do?" I said. "How do I protect myself from hurricane season?" My time clean was short enough that life fucked up still felt very close. I remembered it clearly, a lot more clearly than I had when I was drinking, and I was willing to do anything to keep it at bay.

You smiled. "Go where it's warm," you said, rubbing your hands in front of your new fire. "Meetings. Safe spots. Places with me."

The city was gray beneath me: the sky, the buildings, the streets, the water. I could almost see the death on each whitecap in the choppy tips of the river, the way the city and the winter called to those who might want to die. Each building held a secret, a bar, a drug, an addict. A potential death that wanted to happen. But the cold inside me—I could feel it beginning to melt. It hurt, the way my hands hurt when I've been out in the snow with no gloves and I come inside and it feels like they're on fire.

"Come sit by me," you said. "Come sit by the fire."

Your eyes glowed with fever; your hands open and out, wanting me. Fifteen years sober and yet you were still sick and desperate. It was all the same, but now your drug had a pulse.

I knew right then I'd survive hurricane season. And I knew I should do it alone.

So I took your hand and I held it for a moment, but then I let it go.

# FEAR

# MENTAL ILLNESS ON A WEEKDAY

These days, and I do what I should. I eat breakfast, I get enough sleep, I wash my hair. When I'm troubled, I tell someone who has felt like me. When I'm agitated, I close my eyes, take deep breaths, and treat my thoughts like clouds. I don't do drugs anymore, even though sometimes I'd like to. I have a man who loves me, and I've never thrown anything at this one, besides a bucket or two of sharp words.

Sometimes, things line up in an odd way; maybe it's the shifting of the planets or moon. The chemicals become unbalanced and, like a scale, I can feel it. The weight shifts around on the platform and I become unglued.

In the mirror, my pupils are wet and black like a lake. My thoughts come quick and brilliant, too painful to take in at once. I want to argue about unarguable things, like the Nature of Society and God. No one will win. I can't sleep without the pills.

In the morning, the brilliance is gone and all that remains is the hard, fragile edges. My insides feel smoky. I break the lamp, but that was an accident.

I enter the subway. I'd like to let myself boil over, rip open my chest, but people expect so much of me and there's no room in this world to let it go. I am afraid, because I want to do something questionable. I want to steal from you, to break you; I want to kiss you on the cheek and punch your quiet mouth. I want to fuck that man at my work, the mean one with the bad hair, who tempts me because I know he is bad, just so I could ruin the heart of the man who gives himself to me. I tell myself it is because my boyfriend doesn't understand what I go through, not really, but this is a lie; the bad man understands me much less.

The train comes but it has the wrong number on the front and I move myself to the middle of the platform, because suddenly I realize how beautiful it would be to jump. If there were swords in stones with the pricks facing outwards, I would surely hurl my heart at one, just to try it, just to say that I did. To see what it feels like to have something slice me open.

The feeling I have, the flutter in my chest—this has nothing to do with being suicidal. I don't want to die. I don't even want to close my eyes. It's more like this world is not enough for me. I have too much in my heart to be in it.

I don't know what I should do with this, with the boiling going on inside my head. I tell myself it's not real, these are just thoughts, but I fear I might do something stupid. As explosive as I feel, it is nice, too, because I feel like I'm holding onto a secret. I will sit here and brace myself, my knuckles white as my insides burn, and no one will know this fire.

The train comes, and I get on, and the people inside are all quiet. I want to scream at them, to let them know, to show them just what I've found:

That you should cut these strings.

You should cut me open.

You should hunt and slay my pink thudding heart.

Your eyes may not show it,

they might not burn with my fever

but your chest holds one, too.


LET IT OUT.

# POWERLESSNESS

# I DO NOT QUESTION IT

I am sitting in the kava bar with Zachary. We have
not seen each other in six months, even though he
is one of my best friends, even though we once
again live in the same city. I tell myself this is because he just broke up with his fiancée and we are
only there for each other when we need it. But this
isn't entirely true. It is also because he hates making plans and I operate only on a schedule. But my
schedule has been torn down because, right now, I
can only take each day as it comes.

One month ago, I had my first appointment with
a shit psychiatrist, but I didn't know he was shit
yet. Nineteen days ago, I started losing my mind
even worse. Two weeks ago, I was in the emer-

gency room, getting sedated because I thought I could see god and I was swearing at her, calling her a dumb bitch and worse things. Three days ago, Zachary got dumped by his girlfriend. Two days ago, Zachary moved in with me. Four years ago, I got sober. One year after that, Zachary relapsed on heroin, a slide that began with a doctor stupid enough to feed him Xanax. It took two more years for him to get clean.

We've switched places with who's crazier so many times, first me and them him and then me, but right now it's hard to see the difference. We're both sedated—Zachary on Thorazine, temporarily, for the break up; me on Seroquel, long term, for being insane—but the drugs only blot away so much of the glow.

Our friendship is strange and it deserves a story of

its own. How we met deserves a story of its own, too, but I will sketch it here briefly because it will help you understand. We met when we were both very fucked up, in many different ways. Think of all the ways a person can be fucked up, and there— you pretty much have it. We had the kind of sex that is both very intimate and very cold, the kind that leaves marks, and then we stopped talking. Later, like weeks later, and we began to text each other mean and hateful things. The hateful texts led to more sex. This process repeated itself, until one day it stopped. This was all a long time ago. This was back when we were different people.

I once asked Zachary if the fiancée knew that we used to sleep together. He says he thinks she knows but doesn't want to know. Personally, my favorite method for treating our history is to pretend it doesn't exist. Usually it feels like it doesn't.

The kava bartender, who has tinged blue hair and the eyes to match, tells me her spiel about the kava. It tastes like dirt water, is made from the root, and grows in places like Fiji. It does good things: relaxes muscles, calms you down and makes you feel happy. These cups are made from coconut shells. We should cheer them together and we should say "Bula." The slices of orange are the chaser.

Zachary says "Bula," but that seems like bullshit so I say nothing, and we clink the coconut shells together. We drink the kava. We suck on the oranges. We wait.

I was scared to drink the kava because I had never done it before, and because I knew I would like it because it will change how I feel. But Zachary peer pressured me into coming here. Which is funny, considering when I had one year sober, he called me and told me he would send me heroin in the mail because he knew it would turn me into a junkie, like him. I hung up on him and started to cry. This was the last time we talked until he got clean again.

It is not fair, for Zachary, to tell you that story, without telling you that he was instrumental in getting me clean and helping me stay that way—despite and maybe because of the phone call about heroin. When I got sober, my thoughts would get to churning until nothing made sense anymore. "Stop thinking," he would tell me, so I stopped. It worked. It's harder than it sounds but it's easier than you might think.

He let me live with him for three months once, back when I got fired and had no money saved, at a time when I had nowhere to go. On one of those nights, I came home with a busted lip and no bag of coke. Zachary went out and found my coke dealer, took a bat and beat him up.

He can be selfish and prone to histrionics, but he has always been there for me when it counts. He is loyal, and loves fiercely—loves me fiercely—and this is all that really matters.

The kava works and I love it—I love that it calms me—and I love that it comes with a chaser. I love the kava bar, too, despite, and maybe because, the inside of it is made to look like a tree. When I go to the bathroom, I see a cobalt blue ball hovering in the air, and it glows with something that might be love. I tell myself it is not the mania, it is not the kava. It is the truth and it is real.

There is a yoga class going on in the back of the room; the class is breathing deeply and there are weird chants going on. I tell Zachary that this is all too spiritual for me. He looks at me in a way that tells me he used to think that too. Zachary has been busy changing, it seems. Old Zachary would never hang out in a kava bar. But the old me wouldn't, either.

A few minutes later, and the chants go away. A new track begins on the stereo system.

"This is my jam," Zachary says to me.

"Seriously?" I say.

"Seriously," he says. "If you close your eyes, you get the sensation of floating."

I close my eyes, for a second, but there's people in the room and daylight through the door and so they flicker back open. "I want to close my eyes," I tell him. "But I feel too self-conscious."

"Here," he says.

He turns around on his stool, so we are no longer facing the door and the bar. Now no one can look at our faces. We close our eyes, and we breathe deep.

At first it is nothing, and then it is something and then it feels like I'm floating. It feels so good that I do not question if these feelings are real and valid, or if there is simply too much dopamine sizzling around in my brain. I feel like the burden of being troubled, of being human, has been lifted, and I let it lift. I let myself sit there with my eyes closed, just breathing. I let myself feel like a cobalt blue ball.

# SELF-LOATHING

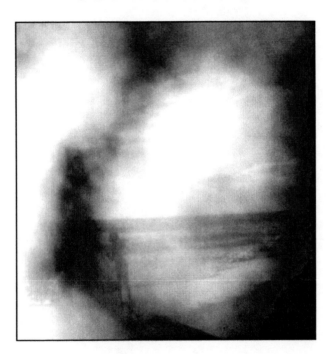

# GRUNION RUN

We decided to watch the fish fuck on the beach.
It was my first date with this good man, and the
moon was waning gibbous. I should have read the
signs, yet I was still hopeful. Before I met up with
him, I coached myself: This is a good man, so I will
be good; no trouble, no trickery, no vexes.

We met at the beach at sunset. He brought a blanket, a chocolate bar, and a bottle of wine. We sat in
the sand and began to drink. The sun sank down
and the air grew cold and he held my hand. He
told me about his day. He told me sweet things,
and quickly I grew bored and restless. So I started
telling him things my mother taught me while I was
growing up.

"The sand will be alive soon, and slippery," I started, because that's what my mother told me to say. "It will crawl, and you won't know where to stand, where it will be safe to plant your feet. The ground will move under you, you will no longer mistake it for a solid object. The air will stink strongly of fish."

He smiled politely, pretended as though I wasn't speaking in incantations. He was new to California, moved here three months ago from the Midwest, so it was alright for me to talk in this way. California is the last place on the map, land of golden dreams, and I wanted to be a dreamer. He may have been a good man, but I knew he still wanted a little magic.

"This isn't the only strange thing the ocean does," I continued. "On the right nights, the sun falls into the horizon like Achilles and flashes green. Sometimes the waves turn thick and brown with algae, it looks like rusted blood, and the city quarantines off the beach from hopeful swimmers. But once it is dark, the surfers sneak out anyway and the crests of the waves glint blue beneath their boards. Bioluminescence, it's called. Living light. Fireflies and jellyfish do it too, but this is better, this is the sea itself, it is more powerful. But sometimes it glows too strong and the surfers can't help but follow it under. Sometimes they dive down and sometimes they die."

I wanted to stop speaking now, but I had already treaded too far. The words tumbled out of my mouth in ribbons, bitter and curling. I watched his eyes glaze over as I spoke. I watched his pupils turn into flat disks, dull and dry as paper.

I was quiet. I was worried. His breathing was heavy

and deep. I hadn't wanted to do this, to say those things, but, like always, it just sort of happened. Time passed, and I let it. Slowly, the good man's breaths returned to normal.

"Where did you hear this?" he asked me, finally.

His pupils looked alright again. I inhaled sharp, a sigh of relief.

"My mother," I said to him. "She's a marine biologist," I lied.

"She compared the water to blood?" he said. "She told you surfers die looking for light?"

"Blood's what it looks like," I said, and took a sip of wine, "and it's true." I closed my eyes, but the moon still glowed through the backs of my eyelids, seared in like a stamp.

He kissed me, and I kissed back. I slid off my jeans

and we made love. Like with most good men, the act was unremarkable. I was pleased, though, because that meant I hadn't gotten into him. Perhaps he was stronger than I thought. Perhaps his goodness was rooted more firmly than the blackness in my words.

It was fully dark now, and the light glistened pale on the flat waves. I could see the fish had come in by the way the light darted off of the water.

"Let's go," I said, and grabbed his hand. "Grunion run."

We ran to the shore, our fingers interlaced, and my heart leapt because I felt like one half of a normal couple. I watched him carefully as the fish fucked slippery between our toes. The cuffs of my jeans grew heavy and wet, and the good man laughed and laughed. I relaxed. He was safe. I couldn't get to him. There was hope for us yet.

I plunged my hand into the darkness and extracted a fish. It flopped around in my palm, telling my fortune like a red piece of Chinese plastic film. If the fish turns over, it means your heart is fickle. Stay on one side, I told the fish, stay true. I stared at it in the moonlight, its flat-looking moon eyes, its leg-looking little fins. I closed my hand around it again, felt the solidness of this fish, felt myself grow lost in the blackness of its gaze. Then its eyes and mine became one. The fish stilled in my hand.

The ground grew unsteady. I didn't know where it was safe to plant my feet. I felt the world under the sand opening from below, vast and ugly and so incomprehensibly dark.

When I looked up again, there was a flash of brightness on the horizon. I saw the good man's shoulders above the water, outlined by the light.

Then I only saw his head, and then he was gone.

# ENVY

# HERE IS A GHOST STORY

My boyfriend's fiancée is dead. Eliza is her name. She'd been dead long before I met David, but still she comes around.

Yesterday was All Soul's Day, so he went out to the graveyard in Queens to pay his respects. It was cold, one of those days with the sky so grey it looks like it's been baked in lint. The kind that confines you, makes it hard to breathe. The trees hang crooked and thin this time of year.

I wasn't invited, so I lay out on the couch while he's gone, listening to sad songs and smoking cigarettes. Seemed a good time to honor my losses, too.

When David came back, the room was dark and

the needle was skating the edge of the record. "That wears it down," he scolded me, as he'd done so many times before.

"Sorry," I told him, but I wasn't. I liked the sound of a spinning record. Reminds you things still go around—endless circles, endless chain—even when you think they aren't meant to.

He sat down on the coffee table in front of me. I hadn't yet bothered to get up. He still hadn't taken off his gloves, and there was mud on his boots.

"So," he said, but really what he meant was *What the fuck are you doing?* because I was just sitting there, alone in the quiet dark.

"So," I said, ignoring what he didn't say. "How was it?"

He looked up real quick and then went somewhere far away in his head. When he came back, he said,

"I sang songs to her, cuz she used to like the way I sang. I spat whiskey on her grave and then I sat against the tree and cried."

"You never sing me songs," I said.

"You never asked me to."

And that was that. And then we had dinner.

\*\*\*

The next day on the subway, I was going to work and someone sat beside me, someone that looked like her. Eliza. Same long limbs and same fine hair, same slight smile and same blue eyes, just like I'd seen in the pictures. She sat there next to me, the vibrancy around her humming and doing tricks. This was a nice girl, all clear skin and clean clothes. This was a woman who was nothing like me. She looked whole and she looked happy, and here I was, late for work and neither.

Sometimes I felt I wasn't enough for David, but then I'd remember when we met he'd stare at me for hours, looking in my eyes like he was taking something from me. Sometimes I'd stir in my sleep, even now, and he'd be sitting there and just watching. "You look so peaceful when you're sleeping," he said the first time I caught him.

"And awake?"

"When you're awake," he said, "your eyes are wild." He took my hand, the way he does when he has to tell me some truth. "They dart about and don't ever stop on something for too long, like you're afraid that by looking at things you could break them apart. You could break me apart." He kissed me on the cheek, all tender like he does, and the whole thing was so sweet I wanted to puke.

But if that isn't love, well then I don't know what is. I couldn't bring myself to tell him the truth, that all that darting around had nothing to do with wildness. It was as simple as knowing he'd break *me*. I hadn't the magic to do that kind of thing to him.

The next day, after he'd left for work, I looked in the mirror just to check. There was no wildness. There was no power. There was only greyness, my heart stifled, my expression rolling out flat.

The girl on the train, the one that looked like Eliza, was humming a little tune. I wondered if it was what David sang to her, and if they'd sung it together. It was a nice tune. I might like to hum it myself but I'm tone deaf.

Eliza's nail polish matched her lipstick, and her purse matched her shoes. My nail polish was chipped, and my shoes had busted soles and matched nothing. I wondered what would happen if I told her to shut up.

She got off at the next stop: Wall Street. Eliza was probably a banker—would explain the fancy shoes—not some perpetually broke English teacher like me.

***

I was so mad that night when David got home but he just smiled and stared and pretended nothing was wrong. We drank wine and I drank too much. At one point, I really did feel wild-eyed. I went into the bathroom while he was turning the record to take a look at myself, so empty and wanting, and then I punched the mirror.

David came running. "What happened?" he said.

My knuckles were bleeding. "It fell off the wall.

Cut myself when I went to pick it up."

He acted polite and pretended I wasn't lying.

We went to sleep, together but alone, that night. We did no eye gazing at all. Just stared at the backs of our own eyelids, an act that doesn't take and gives nothing to no one.

***

Eliza came to me in a dream, again. She'd been doing that for a while, but usually I just ignored her. Tonight, she was all white gown and washed-out skin. Like she was dead. We were in Queens and there was a spit of whiskey on her grave. The liquor hung heavy in the air.

"What do you want?" I said, not accusatory, just wondering.

Eliza gripped me by the shoulders and her touch

was cold and then she brought her face to mine. "What are you so afraid of?" she asked me.

I was quiet because I knew she really was asking for an answer, and I had to think. *Everything*, I wanted to say, *it's everything in this world that scares me*, but I knew how dumb that sounded.

Except she was a ghost, so I only needed to say the words in my head. Eliza laughed, all metallic and light. "That's funny," she said. "He's afraid of everything too." She smiled at me. I'd never seen a smile so warm, especially coming off a dead girl.

"Eliza," I said and, by saying her name, her form became that much more solid. It felt good to conjure; it felt good to finally, for once, have some power. I said her name again, and then her fine blond hair blew upwards in the wind. "Why won't you leave us alone?" Her form was fading and it was starting to rain.

It was just me and her grave then. There was dirt on the stone marker, and I scuffed it away with my foot. I still couldn't figure out why she fucking cared.

I woke up right after, and David was curling his sleep-hot body into mine. The light from the dawn made our room streaked with shadows and the darkness licked us, lying together in our bed. He looked so peaceful when he was sleeping, so small, that I thought maybe I could break him apart.

# SHAME

# TROUBLE AND TROUBLEDNESS

## I.

My dad gave me a pocketknife for my eleventh birthday. It had my name on the side and came with tweezers that looked like barbeque tongs for dolls.

One day my mom yelled at me for something that made no sense and so I ran outside. The thing swirled up, the empty black thing, growing from the pit of my stomach, tendrils reaching into my arms. My vision went hot and I wanted to jump into the ocean and swim out far until I couldn't come back.

I flicked the blade out. I wanted to make a heart in

my calf. My skin got whiter as I cut, and then the whiteness filled in with blood. I carved each line three times, just to make sure it went deep enough. The blackness shrank.

I wiped the blood away with the meaty part of my palm. I licked my hand clean. It tasted like copper and dirt. My leg hurt, but I felt tough on the inside, like I could hide the thing inside me. My jeans stuck to the blood but later it scabbed over, and when the scab fell off there was a perfect and even heart-shaped scar.

## II.

When I was fifteen, I had two best friends. They had boyfriends who were also best friends. I had no boyfriend. My friends were sometimes mean to me.

The best friends went away for Christmas. The boyfriends and I stayed in town. I spent the evenings sitting around listening to The Doors. During the day, I told my mom I was going to the beach, but instead I smoked weed in the canyon or went to the house of the boyfriend that lived down the block.

One day we were sitting in the garage, bored. The other boyfriend was there too. There was beer. We drank it. It was warm. There was a Guns N' Roses poster on the wall, and Axl looked sexy in it.

"We should have a threesome," one of the boyfriends said.

"Yeah," said the other.

"Okay," I said.

They looked surprised. I felt surprised myself, but I

also felt like I couldn't take back what I said.

I watched them as they took off their pants and rolled on condoms. The skin underneath was so white. They came over to me, and one of them kissed me while the other took off my jeans. One of them put his dick in me. The other one put his dick in my mouth. It didn't feel good and it didn't feel bad. I looked up at Axl. I looked up at them. We were action figures, or Barbies, and someone was playing with us just to see what we could do. I laughed, with the dick still in my mouth. The boyfriends laughed too. It was like we were sharing a joke but I guess in some ways it wasn't funny at all.

## III.

I was sixteen and in biology class. The teacher was talking about Punnett squares. There were pink and white and red flowers on the overhead, each of them with four petals. I looked away from the projector and there was this big skull floating out of the wall, surrounded by smaller ones. I knew they weren't real but they scared me anyway, because they were there and because they were shadowy and dark. I got up and went to the door. The teacher asked where I was going. I felt embarrassed and afraid so I said nothing and walked out.

## IV.

I got diagnosed right after that. They gave me a lot of pills: one red, one yellow, three whites. Five pills every morning. Five pills is a lot to swallow.

A few weeks later, and I was walking home. I took a shortcut through a field, and the sky was a strange color, not blue but also not grey—kind of yellow. There were crows flying around, making their squawk noises and flapping. The world was about to dissolve, they told me this, and it was my fault. I believed them.

I went home and took the pill bottles and emptied them on top of my math book. I poured a big glass of gin. It looked like water. I swallowed a handful of pills with a big gulp of gin, and did it again and again until there was nothing left. PJ Harvey was playing. I woke up in the hospital three days later. A machine had done the breathing for me and now I couldn't talk.

## V.

I had a boyfriend at the school for kids with problems. He gave me his Adderall because he didn't like it. I liked the Adderall. I liked to crush it up and snort it.

Instead of sleeping at night I read books from the office about mental illness and the medications they give the mentally ill. I learned they didn't know much of anything; everything they did to us was all trial and error, mostly error. I didn't sleep. Instead I read and read.

During the day I got mad and yelled a lot. I broke things. Dishes. The faucet. I threw a glass of milk at a counselor's head once, but I missed.

We were supposed to go snowboarding. I was excited. I was thinking about snorting the Adderall in the bathroom and how fun it would be to fly down the hill. But then the headmaster said she had to talk to me. She told me I couldn't go snowboarding. I got mad.

I went into my bedroom and slammed the door.

There was a razor hidden in my sock drawer. I wasn't supposed to have regular razors, I was supposed to use electric only because I was a "cutter," but other girls had them so I'd stolen some. I ripped the head off, put it in my mouth, and bit down until the blades separated from the plastic. Sometimes this cut my mouth up but usually it didn't. The blades were good this way: thin, sharp, and flexible. But you had to be careful, to not cut too deep, and I wasn't careful this time. My hands were shaking. I hadn't slept in so long.

I cut open my arm, dragging the razor, and then made two more cuts, quick ones. The first was the deepest. It was getting all bloody now. I picked up a sock, to wipe it off, but it just made more of a mess. I took the bloody sock and tried to make a tourniquet, but my arm kept right on with the bleeding. It was doing the pulsing thing, where the blood escapes from your body at the same rate as the beat of your heart. It was getting everywhere now. I didn't know what to do about it.

I went back into the living room and the headmaster was there with the other kids and Janice the counselor and they were all like, *Oh my god*. Janice took me to the clinic. It was twenty miles out, and I just bled and bled the whole way in the van, soaking through two hand towels. The doctor stuck a needle in my arm and numbed it real good and then he stapled it up. There were twelve of them, twelve staples. When I got back to school, the kids said it looked like Frankenstein.

## VI.

I got out of the school and started dating this guy. It happened because we were both on acid and he had vines growing out of his head and looked like Mowgli. I licked him on the nose and the next thing I knew we were fucking in his backyard.

It was a bad relationship. There was no other way to look at it. We fought right from the start. We kept on breaking up and getting back together. We kept on getting too fucked up, and he kept on breaking my things. He kicked my car door in. He stomped on my purse and broke my pager and make-up. One time, I yelled at him and he grabbed my arm and threw me against the wall. In the morning, there were four fingerprint bruises on the white part of my arm, lined up in a row like stones.

It took two years for us to break up for good. What did it was him chasing me around the house with a kitchen knife, saying he was going to slit my throat. I'm pretty sure he was just being dramatic, but it was hard to tell. I called the cops. He left while I was on the phone. I didn't see him after that.

## VII.

I couldn't sleep again. In the mornings, out of boredom, I went to the library.

I would only look at books about aliens and crop circles. I'd wasn't too sure about aliens before, but recently I'd risen into a new clarity. The alien problem was real bad here, what with all the military bases. That's why the helicopters flew over so often at night. They were telling the aliens: look at my big ass jet plane. I'll fucking shoot you.

I learned all about the aliens at the library. I learned about the crop circles too. Aliens liked pyramids, apparently. I liked pyramids, so I carved one into my thigh. People are so fucking stupid. They say cutting is for attention, it stems from pain, it points to a hatred of self. But sometimes you just want to make something on yourself that will never go away, something you shaped, something that will be there forever: a sign for someone else to find.

## VIII.

I couldn't stop doing coke all the time. I hated it, but I just couldn't stop. That's a real shitty feeling, in case you were wondering. My nose would bleed, but still I did it while driving, putting it up my nose in one of those plastic bullet things. I did it off the toilet tank at work. I did it at home, with my boyfriend, with my friend, with our friends, alone. Off CDs and the coffee table, off notebooks and my desk and the bathroom counter and of course

I once snorted it off my boyfriend's hard dick. Every night, the dark would creep into day and the birds would start chirping and the planes would start flying overhead again—we lived right under the path of the airport—and my head would ache, my whole face hurt. In bed, my boyfriend would try and lean his body into mine but I couldn't let him. I couldn't let anyone touch me. I just wanted to be left alone to hurt. One morning he asked me why I wouldn't let him hold me, over and over, until I got up and punched the window. It cut through my skin, on the wrist. Looked like a bad suicide attempt, like I tried to go across the street instead of down.

## IX.

I stopped taking medication my junior year of college. Decided that "bipolar" was something "made up" to explain away the anger and drugs. At first it was okay, I was just depressed. I'd sleep all day and couldn't be bothered to eat and nothing seemed to matter but I did my homework anyway.

Then it got to be summer. I've always been sensitive to seasons, to the turns of the moon. I stopped needing to sleep again. I drove from college back to home after finals. It was so sunny. It was so warm. I was listening to T. Rex in the car, and the music sounded so good.

Things went bad after that. I got real skinny, I couldn't stop talking, and my heart was always pounding, pounding, pounding, ticking off time like a clock. The look in my eyes became glinty and sharp.

I drank a lot, to bring myself down. I'd drive my

car real fast, especially at dawn. You can't get a
DUI when you're driving drunk in the day. The
signs on the freeway fly by when you're driving like
that. The lines in the road look like snakes, and it
becomes so easy to imagine yourself crashing right
into a cement wall—bam—and then blood.

## X.

This was right before I got clean, but I didn't know
that yet. I was drinking too much again, every
night, every day. Everything blended together. The
pills, too, they coated things like my life was behind
greasy glass. The ones I took, they were things people don't talk about abusing too much: Methadone,
Restoril. You can snort the Restoril but you have to
swallow the Methadone. It's a big pill, sometimes
gets caught in your throat.

I'd get drunk at the bar with my friends and then I'd drive myself home. That was when I took the pills. I lay around, slumped against the wall, flat on the ground, flat on my back. Everything turns liquid when you get that high. Sometimes, for a moment, I could feel my heart stop.

Stories previously published:

- "The Other Kind of Magic" – Vol. 1 Brooklyn

- "Reduction" – Hobart

- "Heroin Story" – *Electric Literature's* The Outlet

- "The Sharpest Part of Her" – *Pear Noir!*

- "Hurricane Season" – *New Ohio Review*

- "Mental Illness on a Weekday" – Negative Suck

- "Here is a Ghost Story" – So Say We All's 2013 edition of *Black Candies*

- "Grunion Run" – Everyday Genius

# THANK U 4
# HELPING/LOVING ME

Mommy & Daddy, Alana Howell, Amanda Noa, Amy Haben, Anna Prushinskaya, David Rogers-Berry, Ilana Rosenfield, Jana Zawadzki, Katelan Foisy, Meagan Jones, Nick Henderson, Nina Jackson, Sally the dog, Scott McClanahan, and Sunny Katz.

*This book was powered by Red Bull* ™